One Night One Morning

A play in one-act by Martin Lindsay

Moody Lapcat Books

First paperback edition in 2025.

Design and Cover by Martin Lindsay.

Images by Mike McAllan, Martin Lindsay and Canva.

ISBN: 978-0-6451987-7-5 (paperback)

ISBN: 978-0-6451987-6-8 (ebook)

Published by Moody Lapcat Books

Perth, Western Australia

www.moodylapcatbooks.com

contact@moodylapcatbooks.com

Characters

RACHEL—20s to 40s

"I've kissed enough frogs to know they just stay frogs. Or turn into toads."

Jaded and weary, Rachel uses sarcasm as a self-preservation strategy, pre-emptively pushing people away by default. She is often left to fix messes left by her careless—but carefree—drunken self.

GREG—20s to 40s

"Look on the bright side. You got laid last night! And you know what? So did I! What a great day to be alive!"

A goofy bravado hides Greg's self-doubts about his less than successful love life. Impulsively chases opportunities with a goldfish's consideration of consequences but is an awkward romantic at heart.

BOB—40s to 60s

"The stories people tell me. So sad. And after I've had a few—quite a few—I sometimes sort of … help things along a little."

A dishevelled public servant who has stagnated within his position of authority. Despite an unhappy marriage, Bob is jolly and soft-hearted—fond of a drink, a dirty joke, and a sing song.

JANE—20s to 30s

"You should ring in with your story. You might win a shopping voucher."

Attractive and energetic, prone to excitedly bursting into other people's rooms. Focus is not a strength. Jane has a rosy view of the future, with plans for a perfect marriage that could escalate to bridezilla proportions.

Setting

The entire play is set in Rachel's bedroom.

Rachel's bedroom consists of:

- BED with PILLOWS and SHEET, with BEDSIDE TABLE on RACHEL's side.
- DRESSER with MIRROR and CHAIR.
- DOOR to side of stage.
- Lots of CLOTHES scattered across floor.
- TRAFFIC CONES, GNOMES etc under BED.
- DOONA at foot of bed concealing BOB.
- WINE GLASS on RACHEL's BEDSIDE TABLE.
- RACHEL's MOBILE PHONE on BEDSIDE TABLE.
- LAMP on BEDSIDE TABLE, with BRA laid across it.
- CAR KEYS hidden somewhere on stage for JANE to find, and GREG to never happen upon.
- GREG's BOXERS, JEANS, SHIRT on floor at his side of BED. Also, RACHEL's KNICKERS.
- MARRIAGE CERTIFICATE in GREG's JEANS pocket.
- RACHEL's PYJAMAS within arm's reach on floor by RACHEL's side of the BED.

Production Notes

Introductory music can be synched in as Rachel's Mobile phone ringtone at the start of the play.

Ensure the bed sheet is non-see-through under stage lights. Thread count is the nude actor's friend.

Rachel is pre-dressed with bra and pyjama bottoms under sheet at commencement.

Mobile message and call cues are best done using a sound effect and actor reactions towards the relevant phone, rather than timing live calls.

First Performed

Originally performed as the one-act *"One Night Stand Off"*.

Garrick Theatre, Perth, Western Australia, 2008.

Directed by Danni Ashton and Martin Lindsay.

Original Cast

- Rachel—Jayma Knudson

- Greg—Martin Lindsay

- Bob—Graeme Sharp

- Jane—Gemma Sharp

Winner 2008 Southwest Drama Festival Best Play (Western Australia).

Winner 2008 Southwest Drama Festival Best Script (Western Australia).

Winner 2008 Dramafest Festival Best Script (Western Australia).

Expanded into the two-act *"One Night One Day"* and performed in 2020. Also available from Moody Lapcat Books.

ONE NIGHT ONE MORNING

Double BED with PILLOWS is occupied by GREG and RACHEL, asleep and naked under SHEET.

CLOTHES are strewn about—they clearly undressed in a hurry. The rest is RACHEL's general messiness.

DOONA is a large lump at the foot of BED.

On BEDSIDE TABLE next to RACHEL, MOBILE is ringing.

SOUND FX: RACHEL'S MOBILE RINGTONE.

LIGHTS up.

The caller giving up, the MOBILE stops ringing, followed by ...

SOUND FX: RACHEL'S MOBILE SMS BEEP.

GREG sits up with a start, swiftly followed by his hangover. He scans the strange surroundings, wondering where he has ended up, until ...

GREG discovers RACHEL asleep next to him. Realising, he beams a smile at his success. Warily, he lifts SHEET for a peek ...

SOUND FX: RACHEL'S MOBILE SMS BEEP.

GREG immediately pretends to be asleep.

RACHEL drowsily sits up and groans at MOBILE.

RACHEL
Ugh. Bugger off.

RACHEL flops back into PILLOW.

A beat. RACHEL sits up in surprise staring at the stranger next to her. She winces for the situation and her headache kicking in.

Curiosity strikes—she slowly lifts SHEET for a peek...

...GREG instantly snatches SHEET to cover himself.

GREG
Hey!

RACHEL
Sorry.

GREG
... I *was* asleep just then.

Suspicious of his honesty, RACHEL pulls SHEET round herself.

GREG defensively grabs enough SHEET for coverage.

Locked in territorial dispute, hangovers lingering, GREG and RACHEL remain wary of the other's next move.

GREG

So … good morning.

RACHEL

Morning.

Unsure, GREG leans across to kiss her cheek. RACHEL shies.

RACHEL

What are you doing?

GREG

I dunno, really. What do you normally do in situations like this?

RACHEL

I don't *normally* have situations like this.

GREG

No. I'm sure you don't.

RACHEL

Obviously, I could if I wanted to.

GREG

Obviously. And obviously you wanted to with me last night.

RACHEL

That's less obvious. But I don't normally do *this* on a regular basis. Semi-regular, at most. *Occasionally* even. Not that there's anything wrong if it was often—not that it was—as it's my choice and not something to feel guilty about if I did. Only I didn't. And I don't. Not *often* anyway. A *normal* number of times. Statistically speaking.

GREG stares blankly, having lost track long ago.

GREG

... okay.

RACHEL

Do you? "Normally"?

GREG

Hardly ever. More's the pity.

No appropriate words spring to hungover minds.

GREG

A bit embarrassing but I can't recall your name.

RACHEL

(Unimpressed) Rachel.

GREG

Right. Sorry, I ... sorry.

RACHEL grows uneasy.

RACHEL

I don't know yours either.

GREG

Greg. *(Offers hand)* Pleased to meet you, Rachel.

RACHEL begrudgingly shakes.

They lie back, still nursing aching heads.

GREG

Do you remember anything of last night at all?

They grasp at fragmented memories.

RACHEL

We met at the pub. La Parisienne.

GREG

I think I was at The Crown and Badger.

RACHEL

How did I end up there?

GREG

How did I? I thought I was barred.

RACHEL

(Holding head) I wish I had been.

GREG

Anyway, it looks like we hit it off.

RACHEL grimaces at his understatement, then relents.

RACHEL

Sorry, morning isn't my best time of day.

GREG

Yeah, I noticed.

RACHEL reacts, offended.

GREG

Not that I mean you're ... Just that you seem ...
I dunno ... Not that your hair's all crazy.

RACHEL instantly tends her bed hair, paranoid.

GREG

No, it's not. Well, it is. I just meant ... I should
just go, shouldn't I?

RACHEL

You should. Then we forget this ever happened.

GREG

We already have, haven't we?

GREG begins climbing out of BED.

RACHEL

Quietly! Things are bad enough without waking
my housemate and explaining you to her.

GREG

(Turns back, interested) Her?

RACHEL glares.

GREG

Just going.

GREG stands, clutching SHEET to cover himself. RACHEL grips her end to avoid being unveiled.

GREG tugs his way. RACHEL determinedly tugs back.

Stalemate, the SHEET held taut between them.

GREG grabs PILLOW to cover himself, lets SHEET go. He scans the room, locating his BOXERS on floor.

RACHEL is watching. GREG glares a "do you mind?"

RACHEL shrugs and keeps watching.

GREG tries scooping BOXERS with his feet, without success.

No other resort, GREG bends over to grab BOXERS, clutching PILLOW. RACHEL recoils from what she sees.

Mission accomplished, GREG considers logistics of donning BOXERS while concealing with PILLOW. RACHEL resumes watching.

Carefully, GREG steps into BOXERS, pulls them over PILLOW, then withdraws PILLOW. He strikes a victory pose for RACHEL's benefit. She is less than impressed.

He sniffs PILLOW, grimaces, then tosses it back onto BED.

SOUND FX: RACHEL'S MOBILE SMS BEEP.

RACHEL retrieves MOBILE to check messages. GREG locates his JEANS and continues to dress.

RACHEL
It's been going off all morning.

GREG
Sorry. Had a curry last night.

RACHEL
My phone.

RACHEL ruffles SHEET for odours, then frowns at MOBILE.

RACHEL
"Tell me you're kidding. ROTFL."

GREG
Rolling on the floor laughing.

RACHEL
I know what it means. I'm confused why she is.

GREG
Poor sense of balance?

RACHEL scrolls MOBILE, while GREG dons SHIRT from floor. He notices KNICKERS, slyly grabbing them as conversation continues.

RACHEL

It's one huge conversation thread from seemingly everyone I know. "Yeah, right!". Right what?

GREG

Sounds like you have weird friends.

RACHEL

They couldn't all have sent drunken messages through the night.

GREG

Maybe you sent out some drunken message and they're all responding. You were pretty pickled.

RACHEL looks up to appraise him critically. GREG whirls round innocently, covertly stuffing KNICKERS in pocket.

RACHEL

I certainly was.

SOUND FX: RACHEL'S MOBILE SMS BEEP.

RACHEL

(Frustrated) It goes back to the end when a new one comes in! "When when when? Ha ha ha." *(Exasperated at MOBILE)* What what what?

GREG tidies himself in DRESSER MIRROR. RACHEL laboriously scrolls MOBILE.

GREG

Maybe you were boasting about the *hunk* you were taking home.

RACHEL

Sure. Who wouldn't tell the world they'd picked up some random at the pub again.

GREG

Again?

RACHEL

At all.

GREG raises eyebrow. RACHEL resumes scrolling.

GREG

You probably couldn't control yourself.

GREG poses in MIRROR.

GREG

"Picked me up *such* a hot guy! Piercing eyes, rippling muscles, manly stubble." Oh, pimple.

GREG leans forward, squeezes cheek.

GREG

Eww. Sorry.

GREG wipes MIRROR from subsequent mess.

RACHEL

So how did I end up coming home with you
instead?

GREG

You felt compelled to tell everyone how lucky
you'd struck.

RACHEL

Or complaining about the annoying git pestering
me at the pub.

GREG

"So, I slept with him. That'll put him off the
scent."

RACHEL

Who's *still* pestering me the next day.

Taking the hint, GREG pats his pockets, then scans the room.

GREG

You seen my keys?

RACHEL

Of course I haven't.

GREG

Can you see anything in this mess?

RACHEL

I've seen more than enough of you.

GREG gets on all fours—his head aches from the change in altitude— then searches among scattered CLOTHES.

SOUND FX: RACHEL'S MOBILE SMS BEEP.

RACHEL
For fuck's sake. *(Laboriously scrolls MOBILE)*

GREG
Just an occasional vacuum, that's all I'm saying.

RACHEL
What did we even talk about last night?

GREG has steadily made his way to RACHEL's side of the bed.

GREG
I dunno. Poetry? Philosophy? The cure for world hunger?

GREG looks up, aligned for a direct eyeline to RACHEL's chest.

GREG
I didn't go on about your boobs, did I?

RACHEL
Because, how you managed to talk me into …
(Clasps SHEET to chest) What did you say about my boobs?

GREG
I said they were great.

RACHEL

What, so the rest of me doesn't matter?

GREG

The rest of you was great too. As well as your
boobs. Only I've got to know them … know *you*
now. And found out there's *way* more to you. To
know about. Not meaning your … *(Motions breasts)*.
Or that you're … *(Motions overweight)*. Where'd you
say those keys were?

GREG hastily crawls away.

RACHEL

Why were you at the pub anyway?

GREG

Does there ever really need to be a reason?

RACHEL

Weren't you with a buck's night? *(Recollection)*
That's how we got talking.

GREG

(Evasive) Possibly. You were all stroppy about a
wedding or something.

RACHEL

That was the reason I was drinking.

GREG sits up, warily scanning round for an angry fiancée.

GREG

You're getting married?

RACHEL

No. Did you listen to anything I said last night?

GREG

Sure. You were down in the dumps about your job, or your shoes or something.

RACHEL

I was getting drunk after yet another phone call from my parents about the lack of any remotely eligible men in my life whatsoever.

GREG

Ahem!

GREG strikes manly pose. RACHEL stares at him.

RACHEL

Whatsoever. How I'm too picky, followed by the usual hints I should be married by my age.

GREG

That's pretty rough. You couldn't be any older than what, 36?

RACHEL

No. I couldn't be.

GREG

It's so hard to tell in the morning light. I mean,

no one ever looks their best at ... Keys. Keys.

GREG searches away from RACHEL's glare.

RACHEL notices BRA draped over BEDSIDE LAMP. Wrapped in SHEET, she tries to put BRA on.

GREG begins watching. RACHEL pulls a "Do you mind?" face. GREG shrugs and keeps watching.

Beneath SHEET, RACHEL performs a series of strange movements. (Pre-wearing an identical bra so only required to raise straps)

RACHEL drops SHEET, BRA in place.

GREG
That was quicker than I took it off.

RACHEL
About the only thing you weren't quick with, from what I vaguely remember.

GREG
Time flies in the throes of rapture.

RACHEL
I wish you'd fly off somewhere rapturous.

RACHEL grabs PYJAMA TOP from floor, dresses.

RACHEL
I was also drowning sorrows over a friend

choosing last night to announce her engagement.

GREG

Good for her!

RACHEL

To a guy that I totally fancied.

GREG

Ooh, bad for you.

RACHEL

Apparently, he's *wonderful*. Perfect, even. Her dream man. Trouble is, also my dream man.

GREG

Ouch. How did they meet?

RACHEL

I introduced them.

GREG

Hopefully not while out on a date with him.

GREG's chuckle fades at RACHEL's lack of answer.

GREG

Ooh. *Bad* for you.

RACHEL

It wasn't a date. Well, not in retrospect.

16

GREG

If I were you, I'd have got hammered.

RACHEL

I did get hammered. And look where that got me.

GREG

(Sultry purr, raised eyebrow) Hammered.

RACHEL is too dismayed to react.

RACHEL

She asked me to be a bridesmaid. I am *so* sick of being a bridesmaid.

GREG

I thought girls loved it. Free booze!

RACHEL

A day squeezed in some sickly-coloured dress, caked in make-up, fending off randy uncles soon loses its novelty.

GREG

Never know, could be your turn next.

RACHEL

As everyone says when you *still* haven't found someone since the last wedding they said it.

GREG

Still … free booze.

RACHEL snatches her nearby PYJAMA BOTTOMS to don under SHEET as she speaks. (Again, pre-worn for simplicity and speed)

RACHEL

I'm tired of smiling and congratulating others enjoying the luck I want, trapped in a torture gown. Then having to explain to all—including myself—why that luck never happens to me.

GREG

You got lucky last night.

RACHEL emerges from SHEET, dressed.

RACHEL

Sure. A drunken one-off hook-up is just the way to find someone.

GREG

Doesn't have to be a one off.

RACHEL stares.

GREG

Keys?

RACHEL

Keys.

GREG

Not to your heart?

RACHEL shakes her head.

GREG

Actually, could you give me a reference? My
mates will never believe me, and given you've told
practically everyone already…

RACHEL shakes her head. GREG nods and resumes searching.

RACHEL's gaze lingers, reconsidering. No, don't be silly.

RACHEL wearily sits on BED, lost in thought.

RACHEL

You look and you look …

GREG

I'm looking, I'm looking! Be patient.

RACHEL

I've been patient. They're either not interested,
not interesting, or stolen by the friend you just
introduced. I'm *over* looking and being
overlooked.

GREG

I didn't overlook you.

RACHEL

You even overlooked my name.

GREG

Who needs names when we wuz crack-a-lackin'!

RACHEL isn't receptive to his charms.

GREG sits next to RACHEL, wraps a comforting arm. Surprised, RACHEL is somewhat touched by the gesture.

GREG

Well, you have my commiserations.

RACHEL

Thank you.

GREG

And quite possibly a significant amount of my bodily fluids.

RACHEL

Thanks. That makes up for all the years of disappointment.

GREG

Does it? Goodo!

Satisfied all's fixed, GREG stands to survey the room for his keys.

GREG

Anyway, nice girl like you. Some guy is sure to swoop down and scoop you up one day.

RACHEL

(Recalls) That's what you said last night.

GREG

Really? Wow, that line hardly ever works. *(Gives an air-five)* Damn, you dawg, Greg.

RACHEL

Believe me, it wasn't your way with words that convinced me to bring you home. Mister I'm-The-Only-One-Who-Can't-Find-The-Right-Girl.

GREG fears what was revealed last night. RACHEL approaches.

RACHEL

(Baby-voice) All sad because your mates left poor widdle you on your poor widdle lonesome. *(Rubs eyes)* Boo-hoo. Boo-hoo-hoo.

GREG

You don't mean last night was …

RACHEL

Oh yeah. Pity sex.

GREG

But pity sex doesn't count! You won't tell anyone?

RACHEL

I will not be telling *a soul* about this.

SOUND FX: RACHEL'S MOBILE SMS BEEP.

GREG

I'm not sure there's many you haven't told.

RACHEL stalks her MOBILE where she left it on BED.

RACHEL

Will you please find those keys!

RACHEL's face falls as latest SMS triggers a dismaying recollection.

RACHEL

Oh. Shit.

GREG

Didn't get your footy tips in?

RACHEL is dismayed even further.

RACHEL

Shit! *(Keeps to one problem at a time)* Do you
remember what else we talked about last night?

GREG

(Sultry) Did a lot of it involve shouting my name?

RACHEL

I didn't even know your name.

GREG

Oh. Maybe that was me, then.

RACHEL

I think we posted something really very stupid.

GREG

Not one of those selfies that shows up our nostrils.

RACHEL

Worse. Look at this.

RACHEL hands MOBILE to GREG..

GREG

(Reads) "What do you mean married?"

RACHEL rubs her head with a groan, memories returning fast.

GREG

Followed by a serious string of question marks. *(Swishes)* A *serious* string. Has this person no regard for grammar?

RACHEL

After the exclamation marks.

GREG

(Swishes) "You can't get hitched in a pub, you silly cow!" That's harsh. I'd hardly call you silly.

GREG continues swishing MOBILE, nosing about.

RACHEL

Do you remember our "idea" last night?

GREG

Shagging?

RACHEL

Before the shagging.

GREG

Tequila slammers!

RACHEL

That's what led to the shagging. One of us suggested the solution to both our problems was a quickie wedding.

GREG

Nah.

RACHEL

While we were still drunk.

GREG

Nah.

RACHEL

Preferably by Elvis.

GREG

(Instantly recalls) Oh yeah. Why did we decide that?

RACHEL

Because he's the king of rock and roll.

GREG

No, the quickie wedding.

RACHEL

Because it would get my parents off my back and stop you crying in your beer about reaching the age where people assume you're gay.

GREG

That's actually not a bad idea.

RACHEL

Turning gay? I don't think they'd have you.

GREG

No, the quickie wedding. *(Purring)* And I think I proved my straight credentials with you last night. My *bona fides*, if you will.

RACHEL

Circumstantial evidence.

GREG

Reckon I could make it stand up in court. What's known as a *pro bono* in legal terms. And I was *not* crying into my beer! *(Looks at MOBILE)* Nice bikini selfie.

Realising he's snooping, RACHEL snatches MOBILE.

RACHEL

What it means is I have a lot of explaining to a
lot of people about something I'd really have
preferred not mentioned at all.

GREG

Bit late now.

RACHEL

It certainly is.

RACHEL gathers CLOTHES to throw onto a pile.

GREG stops her rush by softly clutching her arms.

GREG

But look on the bright side. You got laid last
night! And you know what? So did I! What a
great day to be alive!

RACHEL

Maybe I'm more choosy about the parts of my
private life I expose.

GREG

I liked the parts you exposed last night.

RACHEL shrugs his hands away to continue gathering CLOTHES.

GREG

So, you got drunk and messaged something silly.
Admittedly, to *everyone* you know. Heaven forbid!

You slept with some sexy strange man you
suggested marriage to. Big deal. Who doesn't?

RACHEL

Well, it would be nice to live in your less
judgemental world.

GREG sighs then pats his pockets.

GREG

Better check the damage.

GREG produces items—CREDIT CARD then BAR MAT.

GREG

Credit card—phew! Bar mat. *(Flips BAR MAT,
reads)* Your phone number, I presume?

GREG holds BAR MAT for RACHEL to read.

RACHEL

(Frowns) No.

GREG quickly pockets BAR MAT as RACHEL glares in disbelief.

GREG

Oops. *(Pistol fingers)* Damn. You dawg, Greg.

GREG produces crumpled CERTIFICATE, squints to read.

GREG

What's this. *(Reading)* I, Registrar of Births,

Deaths, and Marriages for the State of … Hereby
certify the Legal Union of …

GREG and RACHEL look at each other.

GREG

I think we stole someone's Marriage Certificate.

RACHEL

Whose names are on it?

GREG

Fuck! It's mine. And someone called Rachel May
McKenzie. Probably a girl.

RACHEL

I'm Rachel May McKenzie.

GREG

You're kidding. Your middle name is *May*? It's a
month of the year.

RACHEL grabs CERTIFICATE, scans the details.

RACHEL

That's my signature. *(Shakes head)* It's a fake. Has
to be.

GREG

Looks pretty official. It has a watermark.

RACHEL

That's a beer stain.

GREG

Signed by the Registrar.

RACHEL

Someone has signed as the Registrar.

GREG

Still signed, though.

SOUND FX: RACHEL'S MOBILE SMS BEEP.

They look to MOBILE. RACHEL sits on BED, covers face.

GREG

No way. That only happens in bad Hollywood movies or dodgy reality shows.

RACHEL slowly shakes her head, more recollection arriving.

GREG

It's not that easy. We have rules here. Regulations. Quarantine. You need a celebrant or someone for a start. And they vet you. Across weeks. And you can't stay drunk that long. I've tried.

RACHEL

Do you remember Bob?

GREG

Was he that drunk old guy who staggered into our table?

RACHEL

Into and *onto*. We told him about our idea.

GREG

Ooh, over-sharing.

RACHEL

Not the shagging. About the quickie wedding.

GREG

(Recalls) Didn't we sing a song together?

RACHEL

A bit, yes. That's when Bob said he could help us.

GREG

I can hold a tune, already.

RACHEL

Do you remember what Bob did for a living?

GREG

Some boring desk job he hated? Government. Signing stuff.

RACHEL

Yeah, *signing* stuff. *(Holds up CERTIFICATE)* Good stuff. Like Births. Bad stuff. Like Deaths. "And luckily for you two …"

RACHEL pushes CERTIFICATE into GREG's hands.

GREG

What was the State Registrar doing in a pub?

RACHEL

Getting legless and abusing his authority?

GREG looks at CERTIFICATE.

GREG

Nah! He couldn't have been. I mean … *Bob.*

BOB suddenly sits up from beneath DOONA.

BOB

Now what?

RACHEL grabs SOFT TOY as a weapon, GREG assumes karate pose. BOB blinks in confusion.

BOB

Who are you?

RACHEL

What the hell are you doing here?

BOB climbs to feet to stand with authority.

BOB

I asked first. And you can start by explaining who you are before I boot you out of my bedroom!

RACHEL

This is my house! You're sleeping on *my* floor.

BOB *looks about then rubs head wearily.*

BOB

Blimey. Last night must've been a right bender.

RACHEL

It was. *(Frowns)* How often do you wake up passed out on the floor?

BOB

(Shrugs) Every now and then.

RACHEL *looks to GREG in disbelief.*

GREG

(Shrugs) Once or twice.

Troubled, GREG *leads* RACHEL *aside by the arm. She shrugs his grasp indignantly.*

GREG

You don't think he was here while we were ...
And might've *heard* while we were ...

RACHEL

I hope not.

GREG

Me too. I don't normally have spectators.

RACHEL

(Sharply to BOB) Did you?

BOB

Did what?

RACHEL

Hear things. Noises. Voices.

BOB

(Looks about in concern) Hearing voices?

GREG

Groaning things like "Greg! You're the best I've ever had!"

RACHEL

You'll be groaning in a minute.

BOB

I don't think so. I'm a very heavy sleeper.

RACHEL

Good.

BOB

Though I do vaguely recall someone yelling "Ride 'em cowboy".

GREG grins, points pistol finger at RACHEL.

RACHEL grabs GREG's finger in a menacing grip.

RACHEL

Have you found those keys yet?

RACHEL releases GREG's finger. He flexes circulation into his finger then continues searching.

BOB

Look, who are you? You and your boyfriend.

RACHEL

He's not my boyfriend.

GREG

And she's not mine.

BOB

(Confused) Boyfriend?

GREG

No, my girlfriend.

BOB

So, she is?

RACHEL

No, I'm not.

GREG

And I'm not hers.

BOB

Girlfriend?

GREG

I'm a guy.

BOB

I'm confused.

BOB sits on BED, shaking head.

BOB

Honestly, I don't remember anything.

RACHEL storms up to BOB.

RACHEL

You should, Bob. Because we are the people you joined together in unholy matrimony while completely stewed to your eyeballs.

GREG shows CERTIFICATE as proof. BOB takes it and groans.

BOB

Oh no. Not again.

RACHEL

You've done this before?

BOB

I really need to leave the paperwork at the office. *(Realises)* Has anyone seen a briefcase?

RACHEL

You carry marriage certificates around with you?

BOB

When I get a bit behind at work. To catch up on the backlog.

RACHEL

In a pub?

BOB

You get lonely working alone late in the office. And sometimes you just start chatting to people. Have a laugh. Sing some songs.

RACHEL

Then legally marry them.

BOB

Admittedly, this is the first time I've stuck around for the actual honeymoon.

GREG

You really take the celebrant thing to a whole new level, don't you?

RACHEL

Just as well you did hang around, because now you can un-marry us.

BOB

What, divorce?

RACHEL

Divorce. Annul. Make un-done. Whatever. Right now, so we can pretend it never happened.

BOB *frowns at CERTIFICATE, holding his aching head.*

GREG

But I thought we'd agreed a quickie wedding would …

RACHEL

Alcohol makes all decisions null and void. Last night was a series of bad choices on both our parts. Particularly mine.

Rejected, GREG picks up SHOES, starts untying laces.

RACHEL softens, approaches.

RACHEL

Look, I'm sure you're … *probably* a really nice guy. On your day. But last night was solely an irresponsible moment, soon to be no more.

BOB

But this is a legally binding document.

RACHEL turns, approaches BOB threateningly.

RACHEL

It's stained with beer. Surely that makes it invalid.

BOB

We usually just pretend it's a watermark.

GREG

Told you so.

RACHEL

Tear it up. This never happened.

BOB

But this is your copy. We probably posted the original on the way home. I have envelopes in my briefcase. Has anyone seen my briefcase?

GREG

I can't even find my keys.

RACHEL

The nearest post box would've been miles away!

BOB

Downhill?

RACHEL

Yes.

BOB

Thought I remembered shopping trolleys. That's probably why I woke up with these.

BOB lifts DOONA revealing TRAFFIC CONE and GNOMES. GREG is smitten by the stash.

GREG

Oh. My. God. Score!

GREG and BOB uncover more stolen treasures from beneath BED.

RACHEL
Where did we post it to?

GREG and BOB are too consumed with their booty.

RACHEL grabs TRAFFIC CONE and shouts through it into BOB's ear, startling him.

RACHEL
(Shouting through CONE) Where did we post it to?

BOB
Oh, to my Registrar's Department for filing.

RACHEL
Simple then. First thing Monday, you'll go to your Registry, bright and early, to stop it being filed.

BOB
But I'm heading away on holiday.

GREG
Oh, where are you off to?

BOB
Lovely little place down the coast. Wonderful fishing.

RACHEL
You are not going anywhere besides your office to fix this mess.

BOB

My memory's hazy, but I recall a very firm insistence of "Striking while the iron was hot".

RACHEL

I don't know how he convinced you to go through with this ...

BOB

Him? You were the one who was insisting.

RACHEL is horrified. GREG winks and shoots pistol fingers.

With a groan, RACHEL sits on BED with face in hands.

RACHEL

I am never drinking again.

BOB

It's alright. Once I'm back from holiday, I'll set off the due processes. It's usually all sorted within a few weeks.

RACHEL

How many times have you done this before?

BOB

A few. Seven. Eight. Normally it doesn't matter.

RACHEL confronts BOB.

RACHEL

So, you, the State Registrar, are corrupt.

BOB

Not at all! Just a little soft-hearted.

RACHEL

Soft-headed!

BOB

The stories people tell me. So sad. And after I've had a few—quite a few—I sometimes sort of … help things along a little.

GREG

Aww. That's quite sweet.

BOB

And you two were so excited. It seemed a shame your love be hampered by a load of bureaucracy.

RACHEL

We'd only just met.

BOB wraps arm around GREG.

BOB

I distinctly remember this one saying I was his best mate. And awfully complimentary of you.

RACHEL

Was he?

GREG

Was I?

BOB

Very much so. Particularly her boobs.

GREG

(*Resumes search*) Anyone seen those keys?

BOB

So, pardon me for trying to do the right thing!

RACHEL

We weren't a couple.

BOB

How was I to know?

RACHEL

It's your job to know! We only learnt our names this morning.

GREG offers hand for BOB to shake.

GREG

Greg, by the way. Real name. Liked the look of her, so I didn't slip her a false one.

BOB

And you would be … (*Checks CERTIFICATE*) Rachel May MacKenzie.

GREG

That's the little missus.

BOB

You were named after a month?

RACHEL

Surely, we needed legal witnesses.

BOB

(Reads) All of the West Morley darts club. And some bloke called Dave.

RACHEL flops to BED in defeat.

BOB

Look, I'm feeling awfully seedy. Can I have a glass of water?

RACHEL

Down the hall, through the living room. And don't wake my housemate!

BOB lays CERTIFICATE next to RACHEL then carefully opens DOOR, checking his way before departing OUT.

GREG hums Wedding March, sashaying to BED, sits next to her.

RACHEL

I can't think of a worse way to wake up to a weekend.

GREG

Oh, I don't know. As far as mistaken marriages go, in terms of looks, personality, sex factor ...

RACHEL *looks to him in surprise, complimented.*

GREG

You could've done a whole lot worse.

RACHEL

Thank you.

GREG

How do you know I'm not a Prince Charming?

RACHEL

I have my suspicions.

GREG *takes* CERTIFICATE. *A thought strikes.*

GREG

Though this does work out like we planned. I've clocked up some legitimacy, and you're one step back from becoming a mad old cat lady.

RACHEL *gives withering look.*

GREG

They don't have to be real cats.

RACHEL

What do you mean, legitimacy?

GREG

(Holds CERTIFICATE) This here is proof of investment in a serious relationship.

RACHEL

For what, twelve hours?

GREG

No one can call me a commitment-phobe now.

GREG carefully folds CERTIFICATE, puts it in pocket, pats it.

GREG

Thanks to this baby, I'm a certified commodity. Social proof. Market value. Not some lonesome flaky guy no one wants. Someone *married* me.

RACHEL

For an evening.

GREG

Someone wanted to spend the rest of *their* life with *me*.

RACHEL

We probably only wanted to split the taxi fare.

GREG

Someone wanted to hold and to *have* me.

RACHEL

It's getting annulled.

GREG stops, concerned.

GREG

You mean divorced.

RACHEL

Annulled. As though it never happened.

GREG

But it did. From now on, I can legitimately *choose* to be single. With all the mature experience and sexual mystery of the young divorcee ...

RACHEL

Annullee.

GREG

They'll try to work out the enigma. "Did she leave him?" "Did he leave her?"

RACHEL

I left you, definitely.

GREG

See, even you're drawn in by the mystery. It's scientifically proven. Girls ignore single guys, but ... *(Holds up ring finger)* ... put a ring on it. Voom! Interest galore.

RACHEL holds her unadorned hand for him to see.

RACHEL

What ring?

46

GREG checks carefully, sniffs, then picks a crumb and tastes it.

GREG

Cheezel crumbs. *(Aghast)* You ate my symbol of eternal love.

GREG gives own ring finger a sniff.

GREG

Onion ring. My favourite. You shouldn't have.

RACHEL

I didn't.

GREG

Anyway, I'll buy myself a cheapy ring somewhere, then let the divorcee string of flings begin. *(Pats pocket)* I got me a ticket to ride.

RACHEL

And exactly how long is this string of flings?

GREG

Philosophy. I like that in a girl. How long is a piece of string? How many roads must a man walk down?

RACHEL

I wish you'd bugger off down a road. Men using the commitment-phobe excuse are usually playboys or whiny single guys. Which are you?

GREG

(*Defensive*) I've had relationships.

RACHEL

Long-term ones?

GREG sits on BED and dons SHOES.

GREG

Depends how you define long-term.

RACHEL

Years? Months? *Weekends?*

GREG feels obliged to admit.

GREG

Three weeks is my record. Rounding up. She was away the middle weekend.

RACHEL

To be honest, I admire her effort to last that long with you.

GREG ties SHOE laces in silence.

Realising she's hit a nerve, RACHEL sits on BED.

RACHEL

I'm surprised to hear that. I'm sorry it hasn't worked out for you.

GREG nods a wounded thanks.

RACHEL

"Don't worry, nice guy like you, I'm sure some girl will swoop down and scoop you up one day".

GREG

Maybe I'm just picky.

RACHEL

Yeah. Picky. That would be it.

RACHEL lies on her front, chin on hands.

RACHEL

That's what they tell me too. Like I have to choose because no one chooses me. *(Sighs)* Maybe in life's box of chocolates, we're the Turkish Delights no one ever selects.

GREG

Actually, I quite like Turkish Delight.

RACHEL

(Zero enthusiasm) Hooray, I'm saved.

GREG

You don't particularly come across as a "soft centre". More a … hard toffee that might take a tooth for the unwary. Approach with caution.

RACHEL

I'm approachable. Aren't I? You approached.

GREG

Didn't we more happen upon each other.
(Corrects) *Onto* each other. *(Corrects)* *Into* each
other. I think we just met.

RACHEL sits up, disappointed.

RACHEL

I am approachable. Mostly. I *am* a soft centre. A
Peppermint Crème. Sharp and refreshing.

GREG

More like a Coconut Rough.

RACHEL

A *Bounty*—hidden but worth discovering.

GREG

You were a Rum Old Truffle when we met.

RACHEL

A *Chocolat Ganache.* Lush, rich and velvety.

Sensing a game is afoot, GREG moves closer on BED.

GREG

And you've ganache-ed teeth at me ever since.

RACHEL

A *Caramel Rapture* then.

50

GREG

Rupture?

RACHEL

Rapture.

GREG appraises this, lying on his front on BED by RACHEL.

GREG

Or perhaps ... a *Mon Cherie Surprise.*

RACHEL

You surprise me.

GREG

I'm full of them.

RACHEL

You're full of something.

GREG

Maybe I was inspired.

RACHEL

Maybe I'm impressed.

GREG

Maybe a soft centre after all.

RACHEL

Maybe. If someone took a bite to find out.

A moment of lingering eye contact.

RACHEL
Even a nibble might crack the surface.

They slowly lean in towards each other, when …

SOUND FX: RACHEL'S MOBILE SMS BEEP.

RACHEL's head flops to the BED, the moment lost.

DOOR opens, BOB pops his head round.

BOB
I think that was your telephone.

RACHEL
What do you want now?

BOB
Would it be totally out of the question if I were
to have a bath?

RACHEL
Yes, totally.

BOB
No bathtub?

RACHEL strides over to confront BOB. GREG sits up.

RACHEL

Go home. Have one there.

BOB

If you only knew the shouting and screaming that would involve.

GREG

Your hot water a bit unpredictable too?

BOB

There'll be plenty of hot water. From the wife, after another night out.

RACHEL

Passing out in a bedroom of a girl half your age.

BOB

(Frowns) I'm not in my seventies.

RACHEL looks to GREG for support, but he's looking away.

BOB

Anyway, I only want a quick one. In and out. You'd barely notice.

RACHEL and GREG look to him, unsure what they heard.

BOB

A wash. Barely a rinse.

RACHEL

No, you'll wake my housemate. And the last thing
she needs to see is a naked old man. Not even the
last thing—it's not a thing she needs, ever.

BOB

You just feel a bit crusty after a rough old sleep in
your work clothes.

RACHEL

Go home then!

BOB

Without a wash?

RACHEL

Yes!

BOB

But I'm making toast.

RACHEL

Who said you could make toast?

BOB

You want some?

GREG raises his hand eagerly.

RACHEL

You're going too.

GREG

On an empty stomach?

RACHEL

This is not a bed and breakfast!

BOB

Certainly isn't. Most of those have a bathtub.

BOB departs, closing DOOR.

GREG

How's he going to eat toast in the shower?

RACHEL

He's not. He's going, and so are you.

GREG

I thought we were nibbling your soft bits.

RACHEL

The box is *closed.*

The moment definitely passed, GREG resumes looking for his keys.

GREG

What's the hurry? In a few weeks' time, Bob divorces us ...

RACHEL

Annuls us.

GREG

Then we go our separate divorcee ways with the version of the story we prefer. You tell it your way, I cash in on mine. At the very least, it's a tale for the grandkids.

GREG and RACHEL look to each other in concern.

RACHEL

Did you use ...?

GREG

I sort of assumed you ...?

GREG and RACHEL look around for discarded contraceptives.

They at each other, concerned.

GREG

I'm sure we'll be *perfectly* fine.

Unimpressed, RACHEL resumes tidying her room.

RACHEL

You might feel validated boasting of a sham marriage in your name. I don't. It's hard enough finding someone without baggage like that.

GREG

I'll change your name to protect your innocence.

RACHEL

Do you even remember it now?

GREG shies from answering.

RACHEL

There will be no stories told of this, changed names or not. Believe me, word gets around.

GREG

You can embellish your version however you want. Add some mystery and allure. Everyone exaggerates on the chat-up anyway.

RACHEL

Are you saying you lied to get me into bed?

GREG moves to a defensive position behind CHAIR.

GREG

… which bits?

RACHEL

I don't remember. Which *bits*? Did you say anything truthful to me last night?

GREG

I dunno, I don't remember either.

RACHEL takes out frustrations on fluffing PILLOWS.

RACHEL

I'm not using this debacle as some gimmick to get my leg over.

GREG

It would keep your parents off your back.

RACHEL

I'm sure they'd be pleased with my drunken marriage to a stranger. It's every parent's dream.

GREG

They'll be delighted! I can even pop in to meet them if it helps.

RACHEL roughly fluffs PILLOW with a stern glare.

GREG

Or perhaps not.

RACHEL sits on BED clutching PILLOW in a hug.

GREG

Come on, we're married! You're not the bridesmaid. It'll take a few weeks anyway, let's have fun with it.

RACHEL

It's not taking weeks. Bob is sorting it Monday.

GREG sidles amorously towards the BED.

GREG

Maybe. *(Seductive)* Still gives us the weekend for the honeymoon.

RACHEL

We are *not* married.

GREG

One soggy certificate says otherwise.

GREG slinks on all fours across BED, purring up to RACHEL.

GREG

Seems a shame to waste the opportunity.

RACHEL turns, meeting GREG eye to eye.

RACHEL

If you wish to remain the biological male in our coupling, you'll think your next move *very carefully.*

A beat, then GREG warily backtracks off BED, onto CHAIR.

GREG

We're still married though. Think of it as a road-test. See how it corners, fiddle with the controls. *(Suggestive)* Take her out for a spin.

RACHEL

You know what you can take a spin on?

RACHEL throws PILLOW into place, resumes making BED.

GREG

And what a break from solo stress! Single people die younger, you know. Wearing themselves out, putting on a show for any off-chance they meet. But get hitched, you can relax. Let it all go a bit.

GREG sags his belly, pats his gut.

RACHEL

That's quite the prize for any future wife.

GREG

She can pop on a few pounds if she likes. All the more lovin' to grab hold of.

GREG gives RACHEL a wink.

RACHEL

Great! Slipping standards—there's something to look forward to.

GREG

Slipping into something more comfortable.

RACHEL

I'm not settling into some survival of the fattest, whose only shared interest is a television remote. There must be better than apathetic convenience.

GREG

If you can find it. If not, given time, "near enough" could become something great.

RACHEL

No offence, Greg, but I've kissed enough frogs to know they just stay frogs. Or turn into toads.

GREG shrugs off the insult. RACHEL continues tidying.

GREG

Of course, in some countries, this sort of thing happens all the time.

RACHEL

Drunken regrettable bonking?

GREG

Arranged marriages where the newlyweds don't meet till their wedding. Those work out fine.

RACHEL

They have family members to filter out losers. Here, sadly, we only have sobriety.

GREG

I wouldn't mind a family arranging their daughter to marry me.

RACHEL

The Addams Family maybe?

GREG

But it can work. Two strangers pushed together with no choice but to make a go of it. Making something wonderful from nothing. Whereas here we hook up with all our expectations, then get disappointed when they're not met. Maybe we've got it the wrong way round.

RACHEL

Are you saying I didn't meet expectations?

GREG

We were too drunk for expectations!

RACHEL flings PILLOW, GREG ducks.

GREG

Are we so far from that, with our *unarranged* marriage? Who's to say we couldn't make something wonderful from nothing too?

RACHEL

Common sense and practically everyone.

RACHEL sits on end of BED.

GREG

But it is nice though, when it does work.

GREG draws near, sliding onto BED.

GREG

Till death do us part. In sickness and in health.

GREG slides closer to RACHEL.

GREG

Two as one, sharing all that life throws our way.

GREG leans in slowly.

GREG

Love over time. Real love, not just shagging. Nurtured. Evolving. The real thing.

RACHEL

You are not sleeping with me again so don't even try the sensitive stuff.

GREG immediately stands.

GREG

Right, let's get this dude annulled then.

FEMALE SCREAM from offstage.

GREG

Wow. Bob really took that to heart.

JANE bursts in, wearing pyjamas and ugg boots.

JANE

(Points out DOOR) Who is that? *(Points to GREG)* Who is that?

RACHEL

(Weary) Jane, this is Greg, a guy I met at the pub, then brought home after accidentally marrying.

GREG inconspicuously smoothes hair, clothes, and checks breath.

RACHEL

In the kitchen is the State Registrar of Births,
Deaths and Marriages who performed the
ceremony, and I'll be suing in the near future.

JANE

That's a relief. For a minute out there, I thought
you'd really let your standards slip.

RACHEL appraises GREG.

RACHEL

Oh, they've slipped, all right.

Too smitten to notice sarcasm, GREG turns on the charm.

GREG

You must be the housemate?

JANE

That's right. I'm Jane.

GREG

Lovely to meet you, Jane. Sorry, I'm not normally
such a mess first thing in the morning.

JANE

That's okay, I'm not normally so loud-and-
bursting-into-other-people's-bedrooms.

GREG

Cool.

JANE

Like, "Hey, just Jane bursting in randomly again!"
Just something she does.

GREG

(Nods, tongue-tied) Yeah … Cool.

JANE

Bursting in like a mad person. "Heeeere's Janey!"

JANE does "Psycho" knife movements and violin noises.

GREG

(Less sure) Yeah. … Cool.

JANE

Who knows what I might come across.

RACHEL

A restraining order?

JANE

Exactly.

GREG

Cool.

JANE

Yeah, cool.

RACHEL regards them, smiling at each other.

RACHEL

Aaanyway, now introductions are over …

JANE

So, dodgy-old-kitchen-guy—who is he?

GREG

That's Bob. He married us. *(Realises)* Not that it's legally binding, of course. I am actually single.

RACHEL

Not technically.

GREG

But morally, certainly.

RACHEL

Legally *not*.

JANE

Single but married?

GREG

Sort of, sort of not.

RACHEL

Sort of yes-we-bloody-are!

GREG shrugs and discreetly shakes head to JANE.

RACHEL

It turns out our friend Bob out there *officially*
joins people in matrimony despite all concerned
being pissed out of their minds.

JANE

Wasn't that the plot of a Sex in the City episode?

GREG

I don't remember that one.

RACHEL and JANE look to him.

GREG

It's often on in the waiting room at the dentist
when I—ooh, look at that!

GREG is instantly consumed with interest in a GNOME.

JANE

This episode was exactly like you guys. Only in a
zoo. And everyone had beards. *(Thinks)* Maybe
that was a dream. Anyway, a couple on the radio
the other day rang in about their drunk marriage,
so it's hardly a big deal. Wow, cool gnome!

JANE joins GREG who proudly displays the various stolen items.

GREG

That's not all we got, look at these.

RACHEL

What did they do about it?

JANE is too distracted with GREG's goodies.

RACHEL

Jane! Focus. What did they do?

JANE

Who?

RACHEL

The couple on the radio. Did they cancel their marriage?

JANE

I think they just wanted attention. The usual types using a crazy marriage to make themselves more interesting. I mean, how desperate.

GREG

(Scoffs in agreement) Desperados.

JANE

You should ring in with your story. You might win a shopping voucher.

RACHEL

Well, Greg, you might get your wish after all.

GREG

(Not listening whatsoever) Mm, yeah. So, Jane, what do you do? Model work? Actress? Dancer?

68

JANE

Hardly. I'm a just a linguistic anthropologist.

GREG

… Oh.

JANE

Though I guess I do a bit of statistical modelling.

GREG

I knew it! From very first sight, I just knew you had to be a model.

RACHEL

Excuse me. If you're finished chatting up my housemate …

JANE

He wasn't chatting me up.

GREG

I was a bit.

JANE

(Giggles) Really?

RACHEL drags GREG up and aside by his arm.

RACHEL

May I remind you, you're my legal husband.

GREG

You want it annulled.

RACHEL

That is not the point. Well, it is *a* point, but a crap one. How do you think I feel?

GREG

Don't worry, you can see other people, too.

RACHEL

Yes, but you're seeing them in my bedroom. Given what I said earlier about friends stealing my love interests...

GREG reacts to his classification as a love interest.

RACHEL

... don't you think it's ever so *completely* insensitive to cop off with my housemate in front of me?

GREG

You've been telling me to go away all morning.

RACHEL

Yes. But maybe given time to gather myself, weigh things up, eventually finding some non-committal reason to call, like some item deliberately left behind—you know, the traditional protocol—then maybe I'd reconsider.

GREG

I was going to leave something behind: Myself.

RACHEL

I mean a considered romantic follow-up, not

blatant opportunism.

GREG

No, you've lost me.

RACHEL

No. You've lost me.

BOB wanders in with FRYPAN.

BOB

Righto. Found the bacon so who's for a fry up?

GREG and JANE raise hands with a cheer.

RACHEL

Jane, you don't even know him.

BOB strides over and shakes JANE's hand.

BOB

The name's Bob. How do you like your breakfast?

RACHEL bursts forward to break the bonhomie.

RACHEL

Enough! You, Bob—down to your office right now to do whatever it takes to stop that certificate reaching wherever it's going.

GREG

But he's making us bacon.

BOB gives GREG a sly elbow to the ribs.

BOB

I think maybe you two made enough of that last
night, eh?

*RACHEL glares, BOB's chortling dies out. GREG acts innocent for
JANE's behalf.*

BOB

There's really nothing I can do. With my
signature and stamp it'll go straight into the
system. I have a very efficient department.
Especially when I'm not there.

RACHEL

You're responsible, you fix it.

BOB

But that'll need explanations. The Attorney
General might be called in. With my track history,
I could get the sack.

RACHEL

Is that such a bad thing?

BOB

Why should I lose my job for being soft-hearted
to those *demanding* the marriage in the first place?

GREG

We were *pretty* drunk, though. *(Realises, cover to
JANE)* The only reason why I went along with it.

72

RACHEL

You bastard!

GREG

(To JANE) Just a bit of a joke, really.

RACHEL

From what I remember, it largely was.

GREG

"Ride 'em, cowboy."

RACHEL turns to BOB. GREG innocently shrugs to JANE.

RACHEL

Surely you can annul it!

BOB

Not if the marriage was consummated.

GREG

(Worried) Only a bit.

RACHEL

Barely a bit.

BOB

Sadly, getting "a bit" makes annulment out of the question. I'm unsure of the detailed ins and outs, but from a legal point of view, things happened.

RACHEL

So, my marital history gets ruined by a drunken

fling over barely after it started.

GREG

Believe me Jane, there were no complaints at the time. Not that I'm only interested in …

JANE

Bob's right, you know.

GREG

Is he? Sure. What about?

JANE

(Rote) A marriage can only be annulled if there was no act of consummation, one party made malicious deception, wasn't of sane frame of mind, or the celebrant's credentials were suspect.

GREG and RACHEL turn accusingly to BOB. They all then look to JANE, surprised by her erudite summation.

JANE

I read an article on ill-considered weddings. It was called "Oops, I Committed Again".

RACHEL

Off our faces on Tequila cannot count as a sane frame of mind.

BOB

You seemed fine to me.

RACHEL

You were more soused than we were! What happens when I want to get married?

BOB

Again?

RACHEL

Properly. Courted. Wooed. Lavished with attention. Sober. I want a clean slate, not be pre-soiled goods.

BOB

Given last night's efforts, wearing white may be a little presumptuous.

GREG steps in to BOB's rescue before RACHEL explodes.

GREG

How's that bacon going?

Grateful for escape, BOB departs with a wave of FRYPAN.

RACHEL sits on BED, weary.

JANE nods to GREG to comfort RACHEL. GREG shrugs "what do I do?", but JANE nods insistently towards RACHEL.

GREG sits next to RACHEL, putting a hesitant arm around her.

GREG

You're not *that* pre-soiled. *(Glances back to BED)*

Quite a lot of it went over there.

JANE backs away with "eww" face, providing opportunity to step on and discover KEYS, picking them up.

RACHEL

From day one, we're taught to crave the dream marriage. Disney Princesses. Wedding-Day Barbie. Glass slippers. Hurry, though, because you also need to have kids. But don't forget your career! Then work so hard you never have time or energy to meet Mr Right. No biggy. But never fear because your mother will remind you with *every* phone call. You've got to nab your Prince Charming at any cost, without scaring them off with too many … *(Regards GREG)* Rumpelstiltskins along the way. No offence.

GREG

None taken.

RACHEL

Really?

GREG

Why? Which one was I? Oh. Okay, some then.

RACHEL

And you wonder why it matters if the story doesn't go to the plan everyone expects? Magic fairy godmothers can only wish away so much.

JANE

(Wistful) I had a Wedding-Day Barbie.

GREG gazes adoringly at JANE.

JANE

She came with a full-length wedding dress, a carriage with four white horses, and a signed pre-nuptial agreement. Solicitor Barbie had Ken's arse on toast if he set so much as one foot astray.

GREG's interest wilts.

RACHEL

And maybe I'd like my own one day of perfect.

JANE nods, signalling GREG to do something.

GREG

So, in a way, we guys are doing you a favour.

RACHEL and JANE look at him, confused.

GREG

There it is: your wedding day. The one day where you're the princess. The bestest, happiest day of your life. Surely, it's all downhill from then on.

RACHEL

It certainly has been today.

GREG

So, being all cagey, shying away and putting off,
we guys keep that pinnacle ahead for you to look
forward to, rather than looking back knowing
your best ever day has already been. You say it's
lack of commitment, when actually we're keeping
your glass half-full for as long as possible.

RACHEL

I'd like to drown you in a something half-full.

JANE

I can't wait to have a full white wedding.

GREG is instantly transfixed by JANE's happy vision.

JANE

All my family and friends in a big church
decorated in flowers. My dress of satin and lace.
And the *biggest* party imaginable.

GREG

You would look *fantastic*. So, your dad must be
pretty rich, then?

JANE

Oh, he's loaded. He's on the board of a brewery.

GREG's jaw drops with a little awestruck whimper.

GREG

I think there's nothing better than a big
traditional wedding.

78

RACHEL

As opposed to hooking up while pissed in a pub?

GREG

Shh!

Furious, RACHEL stands to loom over GREG.

RACHEL

Don't shh me! How would you like it if I cracked
on to your housemate in front of you?

GREG

Quite a lot really, she's a stunner. Her boyfriend
might have something to say about that, though.
Actually, no, he'd be quite keen to see it too.

RACHEL sits on BED having had enough.

RACHEL

How can I lock the entire world out of my
bedroom this morning?

JANE

Maybe shutting yourself away is the whole
problem. Your perfect man is hardly going to
walk in here and say "So, how about it".

RACHEL

Why not, everyone else seems to be today.

BOB enters wearing APRON with FRYPAN.

BOB

So. How about—

RACHEL

Out!

BOB departs.

JANE

It'll happen for you someday. Probably.
Meantime, you have the next best thing.

RACHEL

Which is?

JANE

You could be one of my bridesmaids.

RACHEL

Fan-tastic.

RACHEL sinks her head into her hands, over it all.

JANE

For the record, though, my wedding is going to
be *huge*. Dad said so.

GREG

He sounds a very sensible man. So, *owner* of the
brewery, or just on the Board?

RACHEL

Greg! Please … keys.

JANE produces KEYS she found.

JANE

Are these them?

GREG jumps up to join JANE. She exchanges KEYS.

GREG

Cool! Cheers.

They stand coyly then GREG realises this is the end of the encounter.

GREG

Oh. … Well, I guess this means I'll be going.

JANE bites her lip and nods.

GREG

Pretty soon.

JANE

Almost like … now.

GREG

(To RACHEL) Though we should swap numbers, Rachel. Just in case Bob can't … After all we've been through.

RACHEL

No.

GREG is crestfallen. RACHEL sighs.

RACHEL

But I'm sure if Jane gave you *her* number, she could pass any messages on.

JANE

Good plan!

GREG

Cool.

JANE

Excellent.

JANE waits for GREG who freezes, unsure how to proceed,

RACHEL lays back with a groan.

RACHEL

Just ask the girl out! Don't mind me.

RACHEL covers head with PILLOW.

GREG

Good point. *(To JANE, still struggling)* Do you need a lift anywhere?

JANE

Okay!

GREG

Great. Where?

JANE

I dunno.

GREG

Exactly the direction I was heading.

JANE

I'll get my bag.

GREG

Except, I have absolutely no idea where my car is.

JANE

I guess we just roam around until we find it.

GREG

That could be a lot of roaming.

JANE

You'd better be pretty charming then. *(Punches GREG's arm)* You can buy me a Frappuccino.

JANE eagerly departs.

GREG delightedly watches her go, then rubs the arm she punched.

GREG

Oww.

Remembering RACHEL, GREG approaches BED guiltily.

GREG

Thanks for a great night.

Head still under PILLOW, RACHEL raises hand, gives thumbs up.

GREG

I hope you don't mind, if Jane and I were to ...

RACHEL's hand signals "OK", then arm flops down.

GREG continues to linger.

GREG

You never know, if she swoops, I might even let
myself be scooped.

No reaction. GREG makes to leave then stops.

GREG

Of course, if it doesn't work out with Jane ...
Given that we technically still are ...

RACHEL's hand points forcefully to door.

GREG

I'd better be off then.

RACHEL's hand wearily waves goodbye.

GREG waves back then moves to DOOR. He stops then approaches BED, takes RACHEL's wilting hand, plants a kiss, and departs.

RACHEL's hand hangs sadly, then drops despondently.

SOUND FX: RACHEL'S MOBILE RINGTONE.

RACHEL sits up, then winces at MOBILE caller ID, answers.

RACHEL

Oh, hi Mum. *Exactly* the person to speak to this morning. … What? How did you hear about that? … No Mum, I haven't got married.

RACHEL crosses fingers on free hand to exempt her from the white lie.

RACHEL

Well, I've no idea why Amy would tell you something like that. She actually lies quite a lot, Mum. And steals things. She's really not to be trusted.

BOB enters with PLATE with BACON then makes himself comfortable on the BED next to RACHEL.

RACHEL stares at BOB in disbelief while listening to MOBILE.

RACHEL

Of course I'd tell you if I got married, Mum.

85

BOB

Lovely bit of breakfast. Bunch up!

RACHEL

Just the tv, Mum. I'll mute it. *(Covers MOBILE)*
Excuse me.

BOB

Oh! Manners. *(Offers PLATE)* Toasty soldier?

RACHEL

I'm going to have you sued, you know.

RACHEL snatches BACON from PLATE, to BOB's dismay.

BOB

I'll sort it out on Monday.

RACHEL

All of it. Without a trace.

BOB

Like it never happened.

BOB waves a finger towards her face, eventually landing on her nose.

BOB

Bippetty. Boppetty. Boo.

RACHEL

Take your finger off my nose.

BOB

Okay.

BOB withdraws his finger. RACHEL resumes call.

RACHEL

Sorry, Mum, I … Yes, I know. Yes, *I know.*

BOB

You know what I think?

RACHEL

(Covers MOBILE) That it's possible to be
strangled with a strip of bacon?

BOB

The legal stuff, the rigmarole … none of it
matters. All that's important is being able to gaze
into the eyes of that special person, every
morning. Just you, just them, and the delight of
being together. Each and every day, for the rest
of your days. To know you love, and *are* loved by
that other person.

RACHEL lowers MOBILE onto her chest to listen.

BOB

I found her, you know. That one person. As
beautiful as the first time I laid eyes upon her.
And each time I lay beside this woman I hold
above all others, I think to myself as I always will
… if only she'd leave her husband, and I could
escape the wife, I'd marry her on the spot.

RACHEL deflates.

BOB

Take your time. Less *over*-looking. Don't rush in
and chain yourself to the wrong one for what will
seem like forever. That's the mistake I made.

RACHEL offers some BACON. BOB takes a piece.

BOB

At least until I learn to forge those signatures.
(Wistful) And I'm getting closer, you know. Day
by day. Day by day.

*RACHEL regards BOB as he munches BACON, then returns to
MOBILE, emboldened.*

RACHEL

Actually Mum, I'll *tell* you when I find the right
person. In fact, I'll shout it to the whole world.
Maybe not by drunken phone broadcast. But in
the meantime, it's probably a lovely morning out.
Just right for a *me*-day. Which means quite
enough of you.

*RACHEL ends the call then swaps MOBILE for the WINE
GLASS with last night's dregs on BEDSIDE TABLE.*

She taps BOB's PLATE in a toast.

RACHEL

To fresh starts.

RACHEL swigs a medicinal gulp then grimaces—it's horrendous.
BOB munches BACON happily.

RACHEL

So, how about *that*.

RACHEL looks to DOOR, but no perfect person walks in on cue.
Her enthusiasm ebbs.

She sighs.

RACHEL

Maybe tomorrow, then.

A sigh, a shrug, then RACHEL swigs again.

LIGHTS DOWN.

END

Props List

- BED with SHEET and PILLOWS
- BEDSIDE TABLE with LAMP
- Rachel's MOBILE
- WINE GLASS
- DOONA
- DRESSER with MIRROR and CHAIR
- Greg's clothes (BOXERS, JEANS, SHIRT, SHOES)
- Rachel's KNICKERS
- Rachel's clothes (BRA, PYJAMA TOP and BOTTOMS)
- CLOTHES RACK
- CREDIT CARD (in Greg's JEANS pocket)
- BAR MAT (in Greg's JEANS pocket)
- CERTIFICATE (in Greg's JEANS pocket)
- SOFT TOY (on/near BED)
- TRAFFIC CONE(s) (under BED)
- GNOMES (under BED)
- Other random stolen items from a drunk walk home
- FRYPAN
- APRON
- Car KEYS
- PLATE with "BACON"

Glossary

Doona—Australian word for padded blanket / duvet / quilt / bed cover, but only if officially sourced from the Doona region of Australia.

Cheezel—A brand of Australian cheese-flavoured snack, ring-shaped with a vaguely finger-sized hole. Lethal in some applications. Adapt to whatever local variation of circular snack.

Bra—Short for brassiere. Quicker to say, still difficult to unhook in a hurry.

Ugg boots—A boot made of sheepskin with the wool as the lining and the leather as the outside. Very snug and comfortable, except for the sheep involved. Usually indoors/bedtime wear, running away from anyone wearing them outdoors is suggested.

About the Author

Martin Lindsay is a Western Australian writer hidden away in the leafy seaside town of Dunsborough.

He is the author of the plays *Spd D8n*, *One Night One Day* and *Brown Acid*, and award-winning one-act plays *One Night Stand Off* and *Past Loves*.

Other plays include one-act *Someone Called Rob*, and finalists in the Short + Sweet and Arkfest ten-minute play festivals with *Couch*, *The Retirement Gift*, *That Little Voice*, and *Possum Play*.

Martin was a contributing writer for *Lifted* in the 2013 Perth Fringe Festival, and co-wrote and directed the comedy monologue/burlesque *Lock-In Love* for the 2014 Adelaide Fringe Festival and 2014 Melbourne Comedy Festival.

Martin's short stories have been included in Black Inc's *Best Australian Stories 2012*, and won the 2013 Stringybark Humorous Short Story Competition, the 2014 Joe O'Sullivan Writers Prize, and the 2019 Peter Cowan Short Story award. His micro-fiction has appeared in Short and Twisted editions and Night Parrot Press' *Once* (2020), *Twice Not Shy* (2021), and *Three Can Keep a Secret* (2022) collections.

He is even known to occasionally blog on his website at martinlindsay.net, when not trying to stop parrots from having sex on his balcony railing.

Martin's debut novel *Wil, Maree and the Mattress* will be available soon from Moody Lapcat Books.

Plays by the Same Author

- One Night One Day

- Brown Acid

- Someone Called Rob

- Past Loves

- Couch

- Framed

- The Retirement Gift

- That Little Voice

- Possum Play

- Third Date's the Charm

One Night One Day

A play in two acts by Martin Lindsay

A comedy about singles and social graces, after a night that went so right goes so wrong the next morning.

Rachel and Greg wake up together, much to the surprise of both.

An awkward situation at the best of times, made all the more awkward as details from the previous night slowly filter back …

Available now from Moody Lapcat Books.

Spd D8n

A play in two acts by
Martin Lindsay

At a speed dating evening at a local pub, five singles consider the question—How much can you really learn about someone in four minutes?

Ahead of them is a night of hope, hell, and free Cosmopolitans.

And maybe the chance to find what they didn't know they were looking for.

*"Hang on. I'm not **quite** drunk enough to make the end of your story."*

"How did you get into that line of work? Did you not study?"

"That possibly came across as a bit needy."

"Polyamory sounds an awful lot like just rootin' around."

"They call me Mike. Rhymes with bike. Maybe you can ride me sometime."

Available now from Moody Lapcat Books.

Someone Called Rob

A play in one act by
Martin Lindsay

Sometimes it pays to just let the call go through to voicemail ...

Rob answers an unknown caller on his mobile.

An angry guy called Adam reveals just what Rob did last night. That's why Adam is angry.

And *everyone* knows what happens when Adam gets angry.

As Rob learns, a lot can be discovered from just a phone number.

Available now from Moody Lapcat Books.

Past Loves

A play in one act by
Martin Lindsay

Ben is having a very good year. It just doesn't happen to be the current one.

Invited to coffee by his best mate's wife, Ben's life … lives … are about to be turned upside down.

And not just by the price of a latte these days.

'It happened before I could stop it. If I'd known where things would go.'

'Where did things go?'

'Where do you think things went!'

'I've heard a lot about you, Ben.'

'This will work much better with open minds.'

'If not completely vacant ones.'

Available now from Moody Lapcat Books.

105

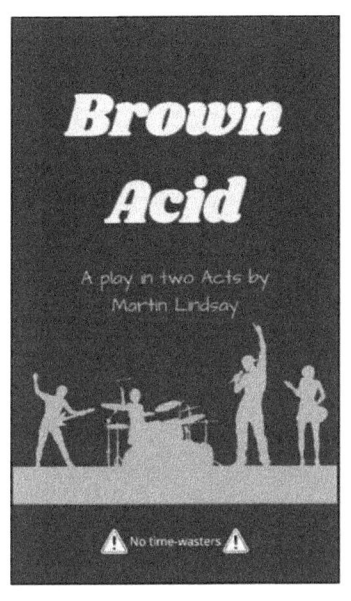

Brown Acid

A play in two acts by Martin Lindsay

Throughout rock'n'roll history, from small beginnings sometimes legendary bands grow ...

And sometimes, they don't.

Wanted:

Musicians to join original four-piece rock band.

Serious gigging opportunities with a group that is going places. Own transport would suit.

NO TIME WASTERS!

Coming soon from Moody Lapcat Books.

Moody Lapcat Books

Books better than belly rubs

Moody Lapcat Books is an independent publisher of books and plays.

Visit moodylapcatbooks.com to see our latest releases, things to come, or enquire about performance rights.

Or contact@moodylapcatbooks.com

www.ingramcontent.com/pod-product-compliance
Lightning Source LLC
Chambersburg PA
CBHW070329120726
47909CB00008B/2662